This edition published by Parragon in 2013
Parragon
Chartist House
15–17 Trim Street
Bath BA1 1HA, UK
www.parragon.com

Rumpelstiltskin

Illustrated by
Erica-Jane Waters

PaRragon

Bath · New York · Singapore · Hong Kong · Cologne · Delhi
Melbourne · Amsterdam · Johannesburg · Shenzhen

Once upon a time, there was a poor miller who had a beautiful daughter. Her eyes were the color of cornflowers, and she had rosy pink cheeks. She was so lovely and clever that the miller couldn't resist telling everyone about her.

One day, the king rode through the village. The miller desperately wanted to impress the king.

"Your highness, my daughter is pretty and smart," he boasted.

But the king took no notice.

"She can also spin straw into gold!" the miller added, sure that this would get the king's attention.

"Whoa!"

The king stopped his horse and demanded to meet the miller's daughter.

He took her back to his castle and led her up a winding staircase to a room in the turret. There, she found a spinning wheel and a towering pile of straw.

"Spin this straw into gold by morning," said the king, "or you'll be thrown into the dungeon!"

As soon as the king left, the miller's daughter began to cry. Even if she had a year to spin the straw into gold she couldn't, for she didn't know how! Thinking about the dark, dingy dungeon, she sobbed even louder.

Just then, a funny little man danced into the room, clicking his heels and tapping his toes.

"Spinning straw into gold is easy as can be!
But if I do that for you, what will you give me?"

The miller's daughter offered
the little man her necklace, and
quick as a flash, he spun the
straw into gold thread.

The next morning, the king was so pleased that he brought the girl an even bigger pile of straw! Again, he ordered her to spin it into gold by dawn.

Well, she still didn't know how to do it. Sure that she would be dragged to the dungeon, the miller's daughter wept.

And just as before, the funny little man jigged into the room.

"Spinning straw into gold is easy as can be! But if I do that for you, what will you give me?"

This time, the miller's daughter gave the little man her ring. Quick as a flash, he spun the straw into gold thread that gleamed in the morning light.

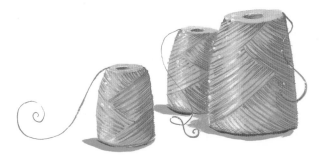

The king was delighted,
and wanted more.

He brought
the girl a
pile of straw
so TALL
it reached
the ceiling!

She was told to spin it into gold by sunrise.

Once more, the girl cried, and the funny
little man hopped and skipped into the room.

"Spinning straw into gold is easy as can be!
But if I do that for you, what will you give me?"

This time, the miller's daughter had nothing left to offer him.
He made her promise to give him her firstborn child. Then,
fingers flying and toes tapping, he spun the straw into gold.

The king was so overjoyed
with the golden thread that he
asked the miller's daughter to
marry him!

They held the wedding
the very next day, and the
miller almost burst with
pride when his daughter
became queen.

The king and queen
were very happy and
the miller was poor
no longer.

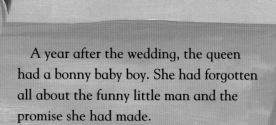

A year after the wedding, the queen
had a bonny baby boy. She had forgotten
all about the funny little man and the
promise she had made.

One day, while the queen
hummed a lullaby, the funny little
man danced into the nursery and
demanded the baby prince.

"Oh, please don't
take my son," the
queen begged.

The little man thought for a moment. Then he clapped his hands and sang,

"You can keep the prince if you play my game—
You've got **three** days to guess my name!"

The queen lay awake
all night, making a list
of all the names she
could think of.

That evening, the little man twirled into the nursery again.

"Is your name Harry?

Or Larry?

Or Barry?"

asked the queen.

But all of her guesses were wrong. The little man cackled with glee and sang,

"You can keep the prince if you play my game—
You've got **two** more days to guess my name!"

The next day, the queen sent
messengers all over the land to
find more names.

Then, that evening, the little
man appeared again.

"Are you named Tim?

Or Jim?

Or Kim?"

asked the queen.

Once again, all her guesses were wrong. The little man
hooted with delight and sang,

"You can keep the prince if you play my game—
You've got **one** more day to guess my name!"

The next day, the queen's servant
was chopping logs in the woods
when he heard a strange sound.
He ducked behind a pine tree and
watched a funny little man leaping
around a fire, singing ...

"The queen will never win this game—
For Rumpelstiltskin is my name!"

The servant hurried home to tell the queen what he had seen.

That evening, when the little man danced into the nursery, the queen pretended to think. "Hmm," she said. "Is your name ...

Doodlebug?

Or Tiddlywinks?

Or Flibbertigibbet?"

The little man shrieked with laughter
and shook his head.

"Do you give up?" he asked,
reaching for the baby.

**"I know ... it's
RUMPELSTILTSKIN!"**
exclaimed the queen.

The little man's face turned as red as a beet and he howled,

"Oh what a shame, what a terrible shame!
The queen knows Rumpelstiltskin's my name!"

Throwing himself to the floor, he kicked his feet and pounded his fists so hard that the boards splintered and split. Rumpelstiltskin tumbled through the floor—and was never seen again!

The End